THE NEXT PLACE

In memory of Tom O.

THE NEXT PLACE

In memory of Tom O.

Waldman House Press, 2355 Louisiana Avenue North, Golden Valley, Minnesota 55427 (Waldman House Press is an imprint of TRISTAN Publishing, Inc.)

Copyright © 1997, Warren Hanson. All Rights Reserved. ISBN: 978-0-931674-32-7

Printed in China. Twenty-sixth Printing

THE NEXT PLACE

WARREN HANSON

Waldman House Press
waldmanhouse.com

The next place that I go

will be as peaceful and familiar

as a sleepy summer Sunday

and a sweet, untroubled mind.

And yet... it won't be anything like any place I've ever been...

or seen... or even dreamed of in the place I leave behind.

I won't know where I'm going, and I won't know where I've been as I tumble through the always

and look back
toward the when.

I'll glide beyond the rainbows. I'll drift above the sky.

I'll fly into the wonder, without ever wondering why.

I won't remember getting there.

Somehow I'll just arrive.

But I'll know that I belong there

and will feel much more alive

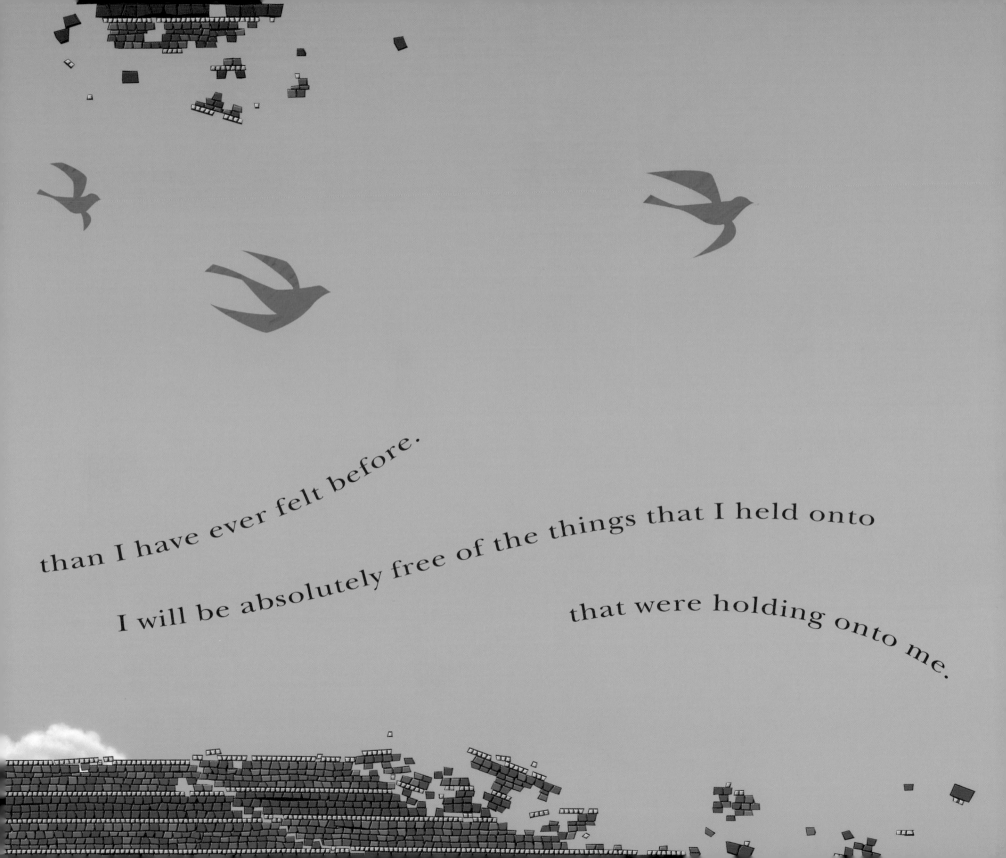

than I have ever felt before.

I will be absolutely free of the things that I held onto that were holding onto me.

The next place that I go
will be so quiet and so still

That the whispered song of sweet belonging will rise up to fill

the listening sky with joyful silence, and with unheard harmonies of music made by no one playing, like a hush upon a breeze.

There will be no room for darkness in that place of living light,

Where an ever-dawning morning pushes back the dying night.

The very air will fill with brilliance, as the brightly shining sun

And the moon and half a million stars are married into one.

The next place that I go

won't really be a place at all.

There won't be any seasons —

winter, summer, spring or fall —

Nor a Monday,
Nor a Friday,
Nor December,
Nor July.

And the seconds will be standing still…

while hours hurry by.

I will not be a boy

or girl,

a woman

or a man.

I'll simply be

just,

simply,

me.

No worse or better than.

My skin will not be dark

or light.

I won't be fat

or tall.

The body I once lived in

won't be part of me

at all.

I will finally be perfect.

I will be without a flaw.

I will never make one more mistake, or break the smallest law.

And the me that was impatient,

or was angry

or unkind,

will simply be a memory.   The me I left behind.

I will travel empty-handed.

There is not a single thing
I have collected in my life
that I would ever want to bring

the love of those who loved me,

and the warmth of those who cared.

except...

The happiness and memories

and magic that we shared.

Though I will know the joy of solitude...

I'll never be alone.

I'll be embraced
by all the family and friends
I've ever known.
Although I might not see their faces,
all our hearts will beat as one,
And the circle of our spirits
will shine brighter than the sun.

I will cherish all the friendship I was fortunate to find,

all the love and all the laughter in the place I leave behind.

All these good things will go with me.

They will make my spirit glow.

And that light will shine forever in the next place that I go.